ZULU THE PUPA

by

Joyce Y. Taylor

Pictures by
Kavion Robinson

Author © 2021 Joyce Y. Taylor
Self-Published: www.joyceytaylor.com

Story © 2021: Zulu The Pupa
The first of the Zulu series, join Zulu the Pupa as he journeys through self-acceptance and transformation.

For permissions, queries or to schedule a book reading.

Write to the publisher, at the email address below @
joycetaylorauthor@gmail.com

ISBN: 978-1-956202-00-7
Library of Congress Control Number: 2021914843

Illustrations © 2021 Kavion Robinson http://www.kavionart.com

MANUFACTURED IN THE UNITED STATES OF AMERICA

DEDICATED TO

My three wonderful children, my three A's, as I call them. Thank you for praying for Mom's book, and the quality time we spend together, and also for helping me to come up with great ideas, and making me laugh in the process. Nothing compares to the mind of a child.

To all the children of the world, coming from all different walks of life. My hope is that this book will inspire you to continue believing in yourself, and know that you have a special purpose unique to you.

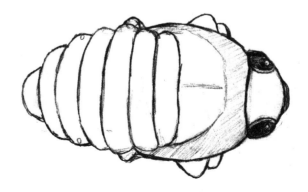

In the land of the rainbow nation, South Africa, there
was a pupa named Zulu. When Zulu was a larva, his
parents told him all the time,
"You will be the greatest of them all."

Zulu really believed them.

However, when Zulu became a pupa, his parents moved away. Zulu was all alone, and he began to doubt himself. He was just a little pupa who couldn't do anything. His future didn't look so bright and it smelled awful!

All around Zulu were insects that were so much better than him. He saw ants, crickets, ladybugs, fireflies, and butterflies.

They were all busy fulfilling their purposes.

The ants worked together as a colony and united, they could do anything

The crickets sang at night. The ladybugs helped to protect the plants. The fireflies glowed like the stars, and the butterflies were the gorgeous rulers of the sky.

Zulu wished with all his might to be a helpful insect like them.

On Monday, he saw Amahle the Ant.
She was very beautiful.
He stopped her as she was walking by.
"Hey Amahle, can I hang out with you today?"

"Yebo!... Zulu," Amahle said, and he followed her
to her colony.
Before Amahle joined her crew, she said to Zulu,
"We are expanding the tunnels today."

"I'll help!" Zulu wiggled excitedly. He immediately started digging away but soon grew very tired, and the dirt hurt his soft skin, he had to stop.

"I'm sorry Amahle," Zulu said. "I wish I could be helpful like you ants."

So he returned to his home.

On Tuesday, he saw Cebisile the Cricket, who always gave the wisest advice.

"Hey, Cebisile! Can I hang out with you tonight?"

"Yebo!... I'm about to meet up with the band. You can join us," Cebisile replied.

A few minutes later, they met up with Cebisile's band.

"It's a beautiful night for Cebisile's symphony," one of his band members said.

Cebisile smiled as bright as the moon and started singing. Zulu giggled, wiggled, jiggled away. He then tried to make his own music, but all that came out of him was **SLOOSH SOSOSOOM.**

Zulu sighed, 'I wish I could be a cricket so I could sing like you."

Cebisile told him, "You have your own unique song. Every insect does."
But, Zulu didn't feel that way.

On Wednesday, he saw Lwazi the Ladybug,
who knew everything there was to know.

"Hi Lwazi!"

"Hi Zulu! I can't turn back, but I'll see you later!"
She said as she flew away.
Zulu couldn't fly, but he wished he could.

On Thursday, he saw a very bright light. It shined boldly in the night. He knew who that was!

"Hey Fenya, the conqueror!"

"Hi Zulu!" The firefly blinked.

"Can you teach me how to glow like you?" Zulu asked.

The firefly lifted his wings and wiggled his tail,
lighting up the dark with his glowing abdomen.

Firefly said, "It's something we feel from within.
A call, a song, a fire, a glow...
Then I say, 'Glow, firefly, glow!'"

Zulu tried very hard to create his own glow, but he couldn't do it. "I guess I can't be a firefly either," Zulu said to himself.

"No silly, you can't. But, you have your own light and purpose in your own special way."

Zulu thanked Fenya, but he didn't believe what he said.

On Friday, Zulu saw the most beautiful of
them all, a group of butterflies flying in a
kaleidoscope.

"I wish I was a butterfly,"
Zulu said.

Bhekizizwe, the Butterfly, the
one who looks after nations,
noticed Zulu's sadness.

"Why so glum, Zulu?" Bhekizizwe asked.

Zulu told her everything.

"We butterflies respect you dung beetles," Bhekizizwe told him. "You work hard, long and your kind are the strongest of us all. One day soon, you'll be grown, and then you'll have your own purpose."

That night, Zulu thought of everything his parents and friends said. It was exciting that he might have his own purpose one day, something that not even butterflies or ants could do.

Zulu closed his eyes and thought, "I'm ready."

The next day Zulu woke up.

He had changed.

The Life Cycle of The Dung Beetle

Stage 1

The Egg

Stage 2

Larva

Stage 3

Pupa

Stage 4

Beetle

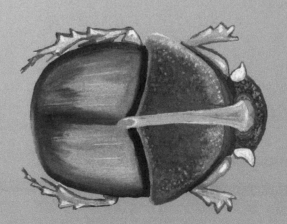

Glossary and Pronunciation of Zulu the Pupa

Amahle (Ah-mah-she) - The beautiful one

Bhekizizwe (Bheki-ziz-we) - The one who looks after nations

Cebisile (Ce-bi-si-le) - The one who gives wise advise

Fenya (Feh-nya-h) - The conqueror

Lwazi (Lwa-zi) - The one with knowledge

Yebo (Je-bo) - "Yes"

Zulu (Zhu-lu) - It means sky, a language spoken in South Africa

Cinquain Poem: Zulu the Pupa

Pupa

Doubt, Fear

Giggling, Wiggling, Jiggling

Journeys Thru Self-Acceptance and Transformation

Zulu

To be continued...Series 2 coming out soon!!

Zulu The Dung Beetle

A Tale of Dung Beetle
Series #2

Endnote Review Request

Dear Valuable Reader.

**If you have enjoyed reading this book " Zulu the Pupa",
please leave a review on Amazon or any platform that
you may have purchased this book. Your review will help
new readers discover my books.**

Thank you,

Joyce Y. Taylor

Author's bio:

Joyce Y. Taylor is a wife, mom, an author, entrepreneur, and motivational speaker. Joyce is committed to changing lives one day at time. Her stories are designed to encourage kids to understand that each one of us has a special purpose in our life. Joyce is a graduate of the University of Massachusetts and earned a Bachelor of Business Administration majoring in Finance and International Business. Joyce also holds a master's degree in Organizational Management and Leadership from Springfield College.

Joyce has over ten years of experience working as a Program Director at a medically intense facility where she manages a diverse group of employees and cases of medically intense adults and children with severely intellectual challenges. Joyce enjoys reading, writing, exercising, traveling, going to church, spending time with nature, and discovering insects. Lastly, Mrs. Taylor coaches and leads a diversified international group of Sunday school teachers. Her mission is to encourage others to always do their best. The first of the Zulu series, Zulu The Pupa book is Joyce's first children's book. More information about Joyce's literary works can be viewed at www. Joyceytaylor.com

ACKNOWLEDGMENTS

Firstly, I thank the Almighty Lord for giving me the strength and wisdom to write this book.

To my husband, Brighton, thank you for believing in me, encouraging me to write, and for offering creative suggestions. The dream has come true!

To my parents and my counselors William, Esther, Noel, Jennifer, Cornelius and Sifiso, your words of encouragement and push for tenacity ring in my ears.

To my siblings, Aubrey, Elma, Queen, Lovey, Dudu, Pablo, Zico, Sanele and Wendell, thanks for picking up the kids from school so that I could write a few more sentences. You encourage and inspire me.

To my great mentors, H.E. Ambassador Uebert Angel and Dr. Shepherd Bushiri, thank you for speaking the word of life to me. You are defenders of the hopeless.

To the children of Enlightened Christian Gathering Church and Good News World Church, you made me feel like a superstar when you heard my first book reading. I will never forget your genuine curiosity and endless spontaneous questions. I will always appreciate all that you have done.

Lastly, to an amazing artist, Kavion; thank you for your illustrations, which brought my words to life.

Finally, I express my great appreciation to everyone who worked tirelessly to ensure the success of this book.

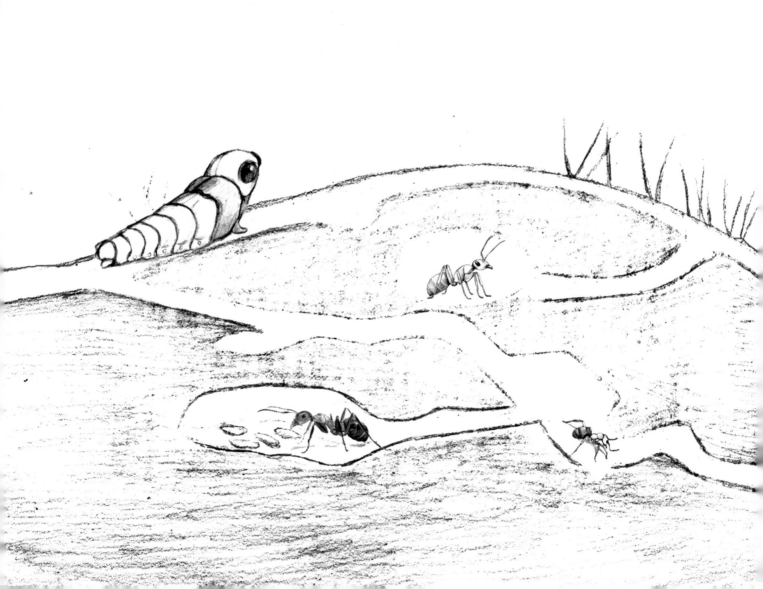

CPSIA information can be obtained
at www.ICGtesting.com
Printed in the USA
LVHW021313281021
701788LV00009B/59

9 781956 202007